PRIG TALES

PRIG TALES

M.G. LORD

AVON BOOKS ◆ NEW YORK

AVON BOOKS
A division of
The Hearst Corporation
105 Madison Avenue
New York, New York 10016

First Avon Books Trade Printing: December 1990

AVON TRADEMARK REG. U.S. PAT. OFF. AND IN OTHER COUNTRIES, MARCA REGISTRADA, HECHO EN U.S.A.

Printed in the U.S.A.

OPM   10 9 8 7 6 5 4 3 2 1

CONTENTS

To my aunt, Anna P. Henderson of Kilgore, Texas, who, for the last eighty-three years, has managed to live a temperate life without ever once behaving like a prig.

PRIG
TALES

Introduction

You've probably seen these people: racewalking to work at 6 A.M. with their personal fitness trainers, downing ungarnished San Pellegrino water at cocktail time, or working the talk-show circuit in their cashmere blazers and tortoiseshell hairbands to denounce nearly every popular television program for its antifamily content.

Or perhaps you know some members of the "Excrowd"—ex-smokers, ex-drinkers, ex–speed freaks, ex-potheads—who were born-again in their treatment facilities and emerged with a mission: to convert everyone—however reluctant—to their way of life.

As recently as ten years ago, these people were jokes. But somehow, when nobody was looking, they took over the world. These days celibacy is in, mind-altering chemicals are out, and the hottest place for meeting singles is Alcoholics Anonymous or the cocaine hotline.

In other words, we've entered the Decade of the Prig.

Just what exactly is a prig?

- a neo-puritan

- someone who says, "When in doubt, don't"

- someone who last consumed a morsel of bacon in 1976

- someone who not only demands diet soda on airplanes, but insists that it be caffeine-free

- someone who shields his or her children's delicate eyes from anything smuttier than "Sesame Street"

Why should I want to be a prig?

- Prigs have clearer skin.

- Prigs are unlikely to contract gingivitus, cirrhosis of the liver, emphysema, or fatal sexually transmitted diseases.

- Prigs tend to have lower cholesterol and higher incomes.

- Prigs can concentrate on their work without the distraction of sexual passion.

But I like the distraction of sexual passion and I believe that bacon is one of the essential food groups. What's the real point of all this prig stuff?

Prigs believe that death is optional. They are convinced that if they exercise enough and eat the right things, they can hang on to their mortal coils forever.

The baby boomers are older now—in or near their forties—and they've lost the adolescent conviction that death is something that happens to other people. What's more, they've produced a next generation. And even if it means renouncing martinis, pork sausage, and double espressos forever, they're d-mned if they're going to watch that next generation supplant them.

But how does that affect me?

If the Age of Aquarius dawned in the 60s, the "Me" generation took over in the 70s, and greed set the tone of the 80s, then the 90s definitely belong to the prig.

There's only one way to survive the Decade of the Prig: conform. Or at least pretend to do so. Prigs are intolerant. If you convince them that you share their values, they will leave you alone. Otherwise, expect them to:

- sneer at you

- thwart your career

- attempt to have you thrown into the Betty Ford Clinic

- and, convinced that they know best, generally screw up your life.

Yikes! What can I do to protect myself?

Prig Tales is full of lessons learned on the front lines of this battle, a guide to help you conform. I urge you to sit down with a tall glass of Ramlösa water—or perhaps a thin, metallic Chardonnay—and peruse these pages carefully. The life-style you save may be own.

Are You a Prig?

Some people have a natural aptitude for prudery. For others, however, priggishness is a challenge to be mastered, a goal to be achieved. These twenty questions should help you evaluate your prig potential. Sit up straight, take your sharpened number 2 pencil in hand, and begin.

Q   1. You are a single female. You would agree to have sex with a married man only if . . .

A   a. his wife doesn't understand him.

b. he is separated from his wife.

c. you become his wife—and then only on Saturday nights if he leaves the light off.

Q   2. Complete this sentence: *I disapprove of frontal nudity* . . .

A
    a. on television.

    b. in the movies.

    c. in the shower.

Q   3. You and a sweetie settle in to watch *Woodstock* on your VCR. As you observe your fellow humanoids ingesting controlled substances and copulating in the mud, do you feel . . .

A
    a. nostalgia?

    b. numbness?

    c. nausea?

Q   4. You are an adolescent male. For weeks you've been having desperate erotic thoughts about the racy head cheerleader who reminds you of Molly Ringwald. You find yourself alone with her in a darkened gymnasium. Do you . . .

A
    a. lunge?

    b. pledge your continued respect, then lunge?

    c. kneel and pray for strength?

Q **5.** Complete this sentence: *I think drug czar William Bennett should crack down harder on the use of* . . .

A a. cocaine.

b. marijuana.

c. aspirin.

Q **6.** At Christmas, a business acquaintance presents you with a bottle of 12-year old single-malt Scotch. Do you . . .

A a. thank him profusely and go for ice?

b. thank him profusely and later, after he's left, give it to the help?

c. tell him he's an agent of Satan and make him watch you pour it down the sink?

Q **7.** A friend has just dragged you to an exhibition of Robert Mapplethorpe's sadomasochistic, homoerotic photographs. At the sight of a vegetable inserted in a predictable orifice, do you feel . . .

A a. lust?

b. hunger?

c. the way you felt when you watched *Woodstock?*

Q **8.** You have just read about Jesse Helms' congressional crusade to eliminate federal funding for "immoral" works of art—e.g., those Mapplethorpe pictures. Are you . . .

A a. shocked at the deep strain of philistinism in the American psyche?

b. shocked that Congress would tamper with the First Amendment?

c. shocked that a dimwit like Helms could have such a smart idea?

Q **9.** Complete this sentence: *The best way to deal with an unregenerate smoker is* . . .

A a. benign tolerance.

b. benign criticism.

c. benign homicide.

Q   **10.** Your close female friend has gotten to be "of a certain age." Alarmed, she permits her hairdresser to color her once-handsome gray hair Day-Glo orange. You tell her she looks...

A
   a. ten years younger.

   b. distinctive.

   c. like a geriatric Xaviera Hollander.

Q   **11.** Complete this sentence: *It is excusable to be caught wearing makeup if you are*...

A
   a. a woman.

   b. a woman with a serious facial disfigurement.

   c. a corpse decked out for viewing.

Q   **12.** Your idea of a yummy dinner is...

A
   a. a charcoal-broiled steak and a martini with a twist.

   b. mesquite-grilled swordfish and Perrier with a twist.

   c. tofu, brown rice, and virgin Ramlösa water.

Q **13.** While flipping channels, you stumble on a sitcom in which a character says "penis" six times in six minutes. Do you . . .

A   a. stay tuned?

    b. turn it off?

    c. organize a national boycott?

Q **14.** You are a happily married woman. Your best friend, however, has the morals of a rutting sow and a string of famous lovers from Wall Street to Wilshire Boulevard. When she calls to chat, do you . . .

A   a. beg her to tell all?

    b. suggest she see a psychiatrist for her intimacy problems?

    c. shun her as a disease carrier?

Q **15.** Sometimes you worry about becoming addicted to . . .

A   a. Valium.

    b. coffee.

    c. exercise class.

Q   **16.** You are a college student with a summer job on Capitol Hill. You discover your congressman—who has a wife and four children back home—is having an affair with a young male page. Do you . . .

A   a. mind your own business?

b. tell your friends?

c. tell the *National Enquirer*?

Q   **17.** A notoriously promiscuous acquaintance has just walked out on his lovely, long-suffering wife who is five months pregnant. You feel he deserves . . .

A   a. compassion.

b. ostracism.

c. to be gang-raped by a band of "wilding" toughs and left for scavengers.

Q   **18.** You think the legal drinking age should be changed to . . .

A   a. 18.

b. 21.

c. 65.

Q   **19.** You are a single woman. A female friend invites you to a party given by her recently divorced, middled-aged "boyfriend." After a five-minute conversation, he asks you for your phone number. Do you . . .

A   a. give it to him?

     b. suggest that he ask your friend to give it to him?

     c. tell him he is a disgusting old satyr and if he were the last man on earth you would join a convent.

Q   **20.** And finally, your teenage daughter informs you that she and her young man have planned an unchaperoned weekend together. Do you . . .

A   a. remind her of the importance of contraception?

     b. tell her that sex is a "sacred experience"—not to be casually engaged in—and remind her of the importance of contraception?

     c. ship her off immediately to a single-sex boarding school in a distant state?

PUT DOWN YOUR PENCIL.
RELAX.

To score the test

Give yourself zero points for each "a" answer, one point for each "b" answer, and three points for each "c" answer. If you went back over the test to recheck your answers before putting down your pencil, give yourself three bonus points, and if you finished in less than five minutes, take three points off your total. Now, add up your score.

1–10 You're a libertine and will probably burn in hell.

10–20 A potential prig.

20–25 Borderline prig.

26–29 Would you like some more Ramlösa water, Mrs. Quayle?

30+ Please drop us a line. You really don't need this book and we'd like to retain you as a consultant on its sequel.

Tipper Gore

The founder of the Parents' Music Resource Center—an advocacy group that works to identify rock albums with pornographic lyrics—Tipper Gore has traveled a long way from her college days, when she smoked pot and took to the streets against the Vietnam War. With her freshly shampooed, Junior League, Talbots catalog look, Tipper is a paradigm of neo-prig style. And of neo-prig contradictions: she shares her bed with a card-carrying Democrat, Senator Albert Gore, her husband.

Eat Like a Prig:

Dealing with the Invasion of the Nutrition Nazis

Prigs haven't been the same since the *New England Journal of Medicine* discredited oat bran. They've become distrustful: not of oat bran, but of the medical establishment. And a few weeks later, when benzene-tainted Perrier had to be yanked from supermarket shelves, they became positively paranoid—convinced that there was a conspiracy afoot to undermine their way of life.

These days, the vast majority of prigs believe that those who are not with them are against them. And since they tend to torment their enemies, the need to conform has never been greater.

EATING IN—
THE PRIG PANTRY

The first step toward passing as a neo-prig is to fill your countertops with cereal boxes emblazoned with the phrase *Contains oat bran*. If necessary, pour the oat bran down the toilet and save the cardboard boxes: they make excellent hiding places for Hershey's Kisses, white refined flour, white refined sugar, marshmallows, potato chips, Oreos, Mallomars, Jujubees—everything you don't want intrusive prigs to discover.

Then stock your refrigerator with several kinds of foreign mineral water, a case of V8 juice, and at least two half-gallons of prune juice. These substances are not as sick-making as you might think: V8 juice mixed with vodka and a dash of Worcestershire sauce makes an excellent Bloody Mary. And if you dump out the prune juice, the brown-tinted half-gallons are perfect for Scotch, bourbon, brandy, dark rum, dry sherry, and other yummy beverages.

Other good props for a prig refrigerator include a jar of Kretschmer wheat germ, a festering bowl of milk-laden muesli, and a few smelly tabs of brewer's yeast.

If a visiting prig compliments you on your well-stocked larder, you must feign ignorance as to the effect of all that oat bran. Although *that* bodily function dominates their lives, prigs blush like schoolgirls when you allude to it. If you can't avoid the subject, however, use words like "evacuation." Forget you ever learned those four-letter Anglo-Saxon terms.

Protein

No self-respecting prig would ever dream of bringing home the bacon . . . or the salami or the pepperoni or the bologna or the bratwurst or any form of meat preserved with that dreaded carcinogen, sodium nitrite.

Few prigs, for that matter, dare bring home meat at all. It has too many impurities: growth hormones, antibiotics, and other chemicals.

Prigs who remain addicted to meat, however, spend large sums of money on the flesh of organically raised beasts: "free range" chickens, as opposed to those reared on farms. And if they still eat beef you can be certain that it is hormone-free beef that they've imported at great cost from someplace like eastern North Dakota. Even then, rest assured that there's still a catch. As one prig of my acquaintance told me despairingly: "I can't get my family to eat it. They say it's too tough and dry."

Another prig employs terrorist tactics to convince her family that vegetarianism is the One True Path. Every time they clamor for a veal chop, she shows them a photograph (taken by an animal rights organization) of a plaintive calf tethered to the wall of an Attica-like cell with a description of the hormones it has been shot full of or forced to ingest.

If they want chicken, she shows them a sad-eyed hen in a squalid coop with a list of the drugs that made it plump up like a feathered Buddha. And finally, if they yearn for fish, she shows them her very own Polaroids of the medical waste that washed up outside their beach house last summer.

Her family members now derive 100 percent of their protein from soyburgers, chickpeas, lentils, and tofu. Her husband has been known to cancel business lunches at the Palm. Her son has been kicked out of the Cub Scouts for refusing to eat a hot dog at a cookout. And her daughter is a burgeoning anorexic. She is very, very proud.

THE FEAR OF FOOD DIET
HOW TO SHED POUNDS THROUGH PARANOIA...

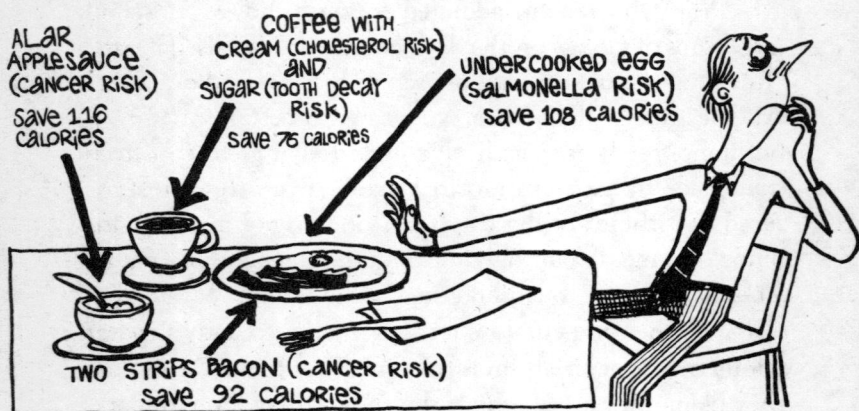

ALAR
APPLESAUCE
(CANCER RISK)
SAVE 116
CALORIES

COFFEE WITH
CREAM (CHOLESTEROL RISK)
AND
SUGAR (TOOTH DECAY
RISK)
SAVE 75 CALORIES

UNDERCOOKED EGG
(SALMONELLA RISK)
SAVE 108 CALORIES

TWO STRIPS BACON (CANCER RISK)
SAVE 92 CALORIES

The Raw and the Cooked

Except for a handful of English prigs who persist in grilling their tomatoes, prigs avoid subjecting their fresh, beta carotene–rich vegetables to the effects of heat. Paradoxically, however, no prig would ever consider consuming an animal product that hasn't been extensively processed. Prigs gag at the thought of unpasteurized milk—and as for meat, they are the first to point out that steak tartare is linked to toxoplasmosis, underdone pork to trichinosis, and raw oysters to food poisoning.

Prigs have taken the salmonella scare to heart. Say the words "runny omelette" and they will run away. And the prigs who aren't afraid of salmonella are terrified of cholesterol. If you want prigs to embrace you as one of their own, avoid eggs. Or better yet, separate the yolks and make your omelette from the whites alone. This concoction not only contains fewer calories but it eliminates the cholesterol and nearly all the taste.

Carbohydrates, Fruits, and Vegetables

Prigs do not live by bran alone. They also swear by bean sprouts, endive, collard greens, kale, kohlrabi, okra, radicchio, romaine, sorrel, spinach, and watercress—by nearly all leafy vegetables except iceberg lettuce, which is notoriously void of any nutritional value.

To create the impression that you, too, are devoted to these colorful leaves, display a bottle of balsamic vinegar and extra-virgin olive oil (prigs love anything "extra-virgin") near the chopping block in your kitchen. Then throw out the bacon bits, Kraft French dressing, tomato aspic, and canned asparagus.

Prigs are nearly as hysterical about pesticides as they are about animal growth hormones. The application of toxic Alar to apples has made the once-popular fruit as appealing to prigs as, say, Twinkies.

Also, when shopping with prigs, ask the grocer if the

vegetables are "sulfite-free." These substances cause severe allergic reactions (like death) in asthmatics.

Surprisingly, prigs love frozen vegetables. Unlike vegetables in cans, frozen vegetables retain their vitamins, minerals, and color. If you anticipate having a prig rummage in your freezer, you should store your Sara Lee cheesecakes, Cool Whip, and chocolate-chocolate chip Häagen-Dazs behind a wall of frozen brussel sprouts. Your fifth of frozen Stolychnaya will be harder to conceal. Soak off the label and advise inquiring prigs that it contains your diabetic child's insulin.

You should also conceal your compromising cookbooks behind a false front of acceptable titles—e.g., *White Trash Cooking, Bar-B-Queing with Bobby,* and *How to Cook a Wolf* should be hidden behind *Your Sodium-Free Diet, Lentils for Life,* and *Recipes from a Monastery Kitchen.*

Leaching

Prigs are enormously concerned about "leaching," which occurs when pristine food is contaminated by its container. It's what happens when you add lemon juice to a Styrofoam cup of tea and the foam begins to fizz into your drink. This is not to be confused with "leeching"—what your ex-hippie brother-in-law does when he comes to visit without setting a departure date.

To guard against leaching, avoid Styrofoam cups and scrutinize hand-made mugs to ensure that they are properly glazed. Whenever possible, sip your tea out of Limoges china cups. And don't, under any circumstances, wrap your leftovers in aluminum foil. Aluminum leaching has been linked to Alzheimer's disease.

ACCePTaBLe   UNaCCePTaBLe

EATING OUT

Ethnic Food

The worst known torture for a neo-prig is a trip to a Japanese restaurant. Soy sauce and miso are full of salt (a heart-stopping no-no), and the fish that isn't deep-fried (a cardinal no-no) is served raw (not just a no-no, but dangerous and disgusting).

Kosher delicatessens used to be torture, but no more. Prigs can turn up their noses at artery-cloggers like corned beef and pastrami, and order kasha varnishkes—the original ethnic roughage—with caffeine-free celery soda and a stuffed pepper on the side. Salt-ridden pickles and sauerkraut, however, remain anathema.

Mexican restaurants would be endurable, except for the pressure to ingest margaritas, a dangerous blend of lemon juice, Triple Sec, and lighter fluid. Worse yet, these Latino Mickey Finns are served in glasses ringed with salt. In American Mexican restaurants, unlike the ones south of the border, water is the *only* thing safe to drink.

Chinese restaurants, by contrast, are prig heaven. If the chef can be trusted to withhold the monosodium glutamate, prigs will find innumerable things on the menu to enjoy. These included stir-fried vegetables (heated in polyunsaturated oil and nearly raw), brown rice, and tofu. But prigs will—and you must—avoid the fortune cookies: they're decadent and superstitious.

Soda Fountains

To the sugar-phobic neo-prig, Baskin Robbins is the equivalent of a crack house, M&M's equals a cache of Quaaludes, and ordinary fudge brownies are just as forbidden as the ignominious "Alice B. Toklas" confections of the 1960s.

Carcinogenic fake sugars are even worse. And as for FDA-approved sweeteners, such as saccharin and NutraSweet, you might as well ingest methadone. Don't even *think* about consuming these substances.

Pubs, Clubs, and Bars

Should you inexplicably find yourself in a bar with prigs, resist the urge to order animal parts that do not exist in nature—e.g., "chicken fingers" and "buffalo wings." Such things are generally deep-fried and served with salt. Slake your hunger with celery sticks. Under no circumstances place a cigarette between your lips.

If you are served an inferior bottle of wine, don't hesitate to send it back. You won't do better on your second because there won't be a second. And don't, even in jest, suggest that you and your companions top off your repast with brandy and cigars.

Finally, forget you've ever sampled the scrumptious nectar of the juniper berry. No matter how priggish your behavior, if a martini brings a beatific smile to your face, your cover is blown forever.

The problem with Shirley Temples isn't their taste, it's their name. In a power-sodden city, like, say, Washington, who wants to drink something named for a second-rate ex-ambassador to Ghana? For sodas that could seriously supplant spirits, why not try:

"The Anita Bryant" – Perrier and orange juice

"The Madame Mao" – Perrier and monosodium glutamate

"The Betty Ford" – Perrier and saccharin

"The Cardinal O'Connor" – Perrier and holy water

"The Kitty Dukakis" – Perrier and rubbing alcohol (or any other cleaning solvent in the house)

What to Drink Instead of Booze

FREE OF RED DYE #2

Betty Ford
(After the Detoxification)

Once Betty Ford was just another First Lady who hit the sauce a little too heavily. Today, however, her name is synonymous with substance abuse rehabilitation. She was the bold pioneer who lurched into Long Beach Naval Hospital, kicked her booze and pill habit, and established a treatment center to help other celebrities (and just plain rich folk) kick theirs.

THE **PRIG** MAKEOVER:

MEET CHRISTOPHER COBURN. HE DRINKS. HE SMOKES. HE FORNICATES. AND HIS DOCTOR HAS ORDERED HIM TO STOP.

HE CHECKS HiMSELF iNTO a TREATMENT CENTER WHiCH USES ULTRA-MODERN TECHNiQUES TO EASE THE DiSCOMFORT OF WiTHDRAWAL.

THERE HE LEARNS TO EAT RiGHT...

OAT BRAN

S. PELL

...AND TO TREAT HIS BODY AS SOMETHING OTHER THAN A RECEPTACLE FOR POISONS.

IN HIS SUPPORT GROUP, HE FINDS STRENGTH, FELLOWSHIP, AND SPIRITUALITY...

MY NAME IS CHRIS AND I AM AN ALCOHOLIC, A DRUG ADDICT AND A SEX MANIAC.

SOON HIS INNER CHANGES BEGIN TO MANIFEST THEMSELVES OUTWARDLY.

PASTIMES HE ONCE INDULGED IN NOW BORE HIM...

MEET CHRISTOPHER COBURN.

How to Dress Like a Prig

Short. Sleek. Sultry. Sassy. Steamy. If any of those adjectives describes your wardrobe, you'd better pay close attention to this chapter.

Neo-prigs believe that frowsiness is next to godliness. Any outfit that turns up in *Vogue* is not likely to turn up on their backs. Frumpy, tweedy, nubby, crisp, starched: these are their bywords. Forget Grace Mirabella; think Mary Poppins.

Prigs love tartan skirts, square shoulders, and those natty emblems on the breast pockets of blazers. In childhood, their boxy school uniforms felt as natural as a second skin—and although they rejoice at the defeat of godless

Communism, they still admire those tasteful gray pajamas that everyone used to wear in China.

This may come as a surprise, but many prigs are into black leather—for their Coach handbags, Bruno Magli pumps, and Filofaxes. If you want prigs to ostracize you, however, try sporting a black leather miniskirt. And if you want a prig's heart to stop beating, strip down to your black leather garter belt. This is especially effective if you are male.

Prig fashion is an oxymoron. The operative word is *protection*—from germs, from sunlight, and from the lascivious eyes of strangers. When in doubt, put on that extra layer. Let's show you what we mean:

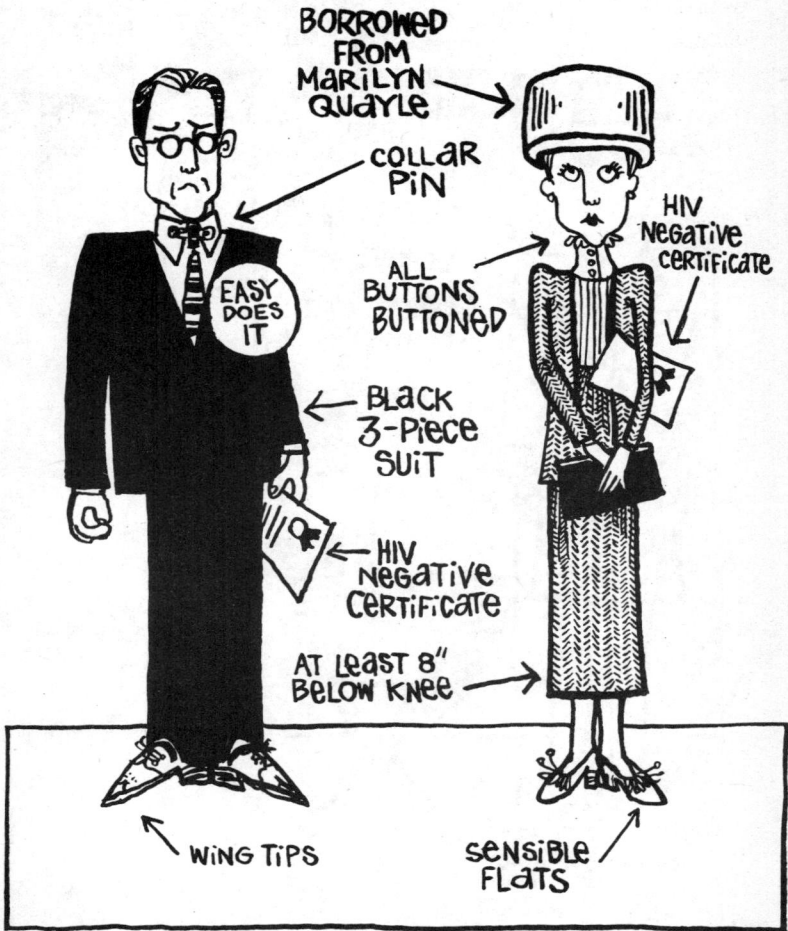

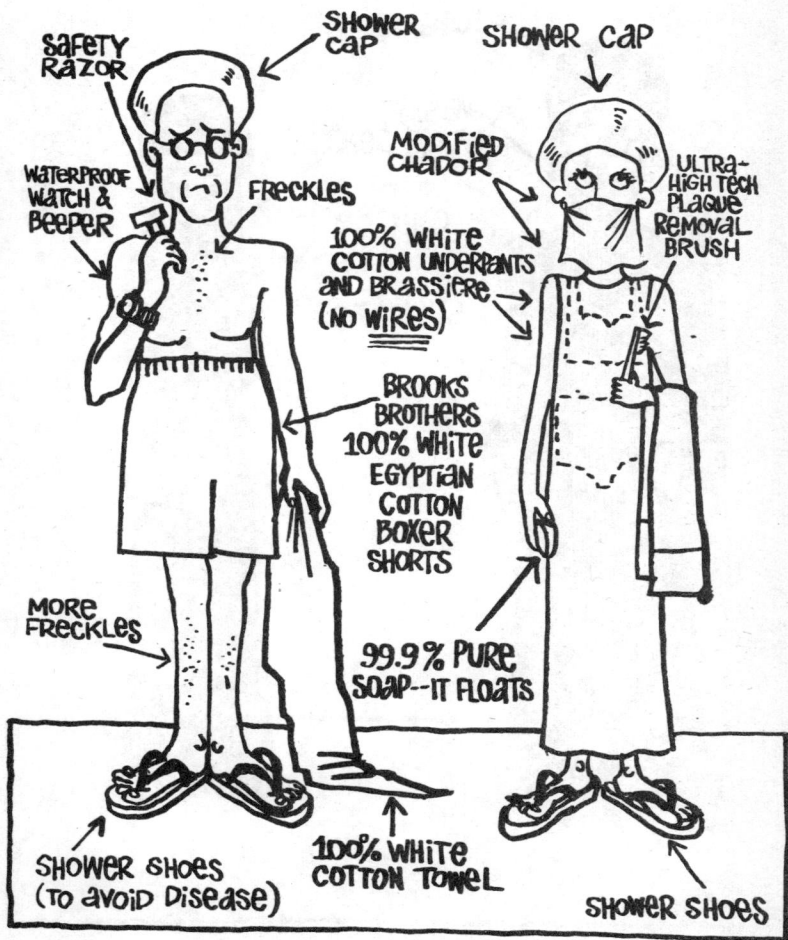

Exercise

At first glance, an aerobics class would seem the least likely place to find a prig, much less a neo-prig. For one thing, the uniform—bone-hugging tights and a high-cut, fluorescent spandex leotard—seems more suited to a 42nd Street hooker than a young urban professional. For another, the music is loud enough to split eardrums and has lyrics which (if they were intelligible) would make Bob Guccione blush. Even the exercises themselves—wriggles, jiggles, and pelvic thrusts—are by any standards obscene.

But because of one irresistible attraction, aerobics classes are prig enclaves: they provide a theater in which prigs can flaunt their superior fitness and make the rest of us feel like asthmatic clones of John Candy or Roseanne Barr.

Look closely at the front row of any aerobics class the next time you visit your gym:

- You'll see people who execute every stretch (bending joints in directions that God did not intend them to bend) and perform every dance step (even ones that defy the laws of physics).

- You'll see people who never sweat or gasp or wheeze or miss a beat.

- You'll see people who bump and grind like Gypsy Rose Lee, then pretend that only dirty-minded people (like you) would consider their movements unwholesome.

- You will, in other words, see prigs.

There is, however, a dark side to all this hopping around: drug addiction. Women who exercise compulsively are very often addicted to endorphins—chemicals produced by their own bodies that give them a high when they exert themselves. True, endorphins don't enrich the bank accounts of any Panamanian dictators, but taking too much exercise too frequently to indulge an endorphin habit can weaken rather than strengthen the body.

If you're being harassed by an evangelical exerciser, get him or her off your back by attending a low-impact aerobics class. The real nuts go to the high-impact ones where, after a period of years, they can be sure to have destroyed all the cartilage in their knees.

If, however, a high-impact fanatic drags you to class, here are some survival tips:

RIGHT

Survival Tips

1. Dress right. If your outfit is lurid enough people won't suspect you're an outsider.

2. Even if everyone around you is leaping into the air like jackrabbits, remain on the ground. Not only will you expend less energy, but your knees and ankles may actually function when you're in your seventies.

3. Invest in the right shoes — even if you never plan to wear them again. A single session without proper support can destroy your feet.

Survival Tips
(*continued*)

4. Unless you're convinced you're at death's door, don't stop mid-workout for a drink of water. The prigs will never respect you.

5. Do stop *afterward* for a drink of water. Prigs often knock back a few Perriers with one another when they've showered and changed. Don't – while in the company of prigs – yield to temptation and order a Jack Daniels on the rocks.

6. Do tell the prig who invited you what a terrific time you had in aerobics class. Feign eagerness to sign up for a class of your own. Then carry a gym bag to your office several days a week and pretend to duck out for a workout.

WRONG

Survival Tips
(*continued*)

7. For another good ploy, pretend to run four miles a day. To pull this off, arrange to be seen on your block wearing expensive running shoes and a sweatsuit early in the morning. If, however, you're grossly obese, this is perhaps not the best ploy for you.

8. Practice using phrases like "Go for the burn" and "No pain, no gain." In no time, they'll roll off your tongue as effortlessly as "Easy does it" and "Let go and let God."

9. And finally, make the best of a bad situation: if your energy flags before an exercise class, what better time to consume a Snickers or an Almond Joy? Just make sure you consume them in private.

Cotton Mather

Author, Congregationalist minister, and driving force behind the Salem witch trials, Cotton Mather has been officially dubbed a "prig" by the *Dictionary of American Biography*. In truth, he was a man haunted by his own demons: although he aspired all his life to be made president of Harvard, he fell far short of his goal and had to settle for the presidency of Yale.

Carry Nation

At age 54, Carry Nation took up her hatchet and launched a national campaign to wreck saloons. A prophet of prohibition, she had until then lived a quiet, ordinary life in her home state of Kansas. Sophisticated New Yorkers countered her loony assaults with smirks, but her antics nonetheless kept the constabulary on their toes.

Jimmy Carter

In an interview with *Playboy* magazine, this born-again president reminded all Christians that lust-in-the-heart was just as sinful as the more demonstrative variety. As president, his low-key, intelligent, profoundly moral style alienated nearly all his fellow citizens and resulted in the Reagan landslide of 1980.

Courtship

Where do unmarried prigs
make love?

a. the computer   b. the telephone
c. the Plaza and the Beverly Wilshire (he's at
the Plaza; she's at the Beverly Wilshire)
d. other

_____

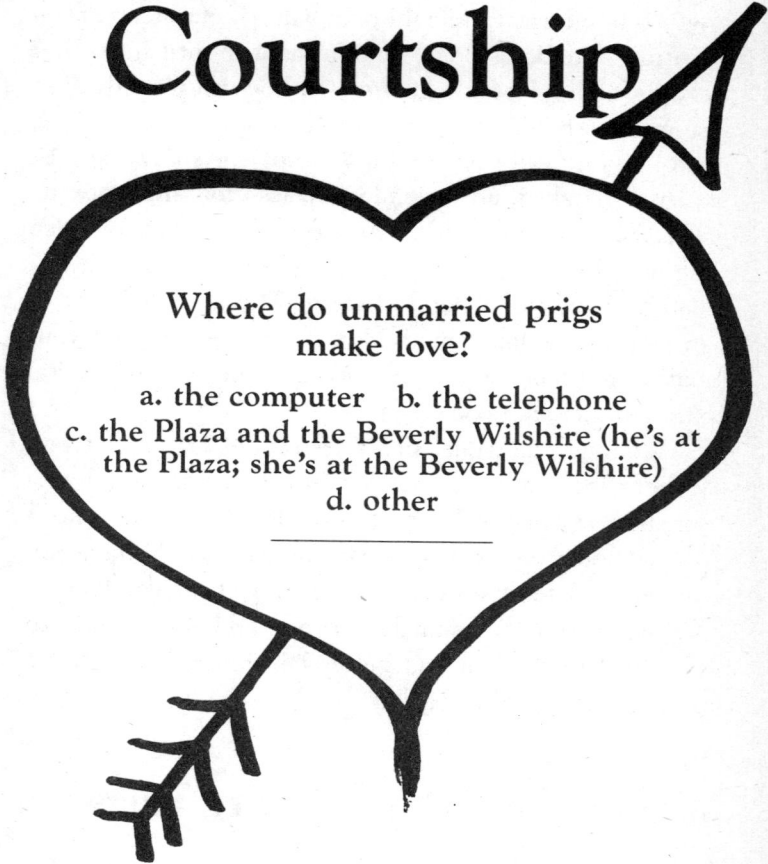

If you answered "a," "b," or "c," skip this chapter. If,
however, you responded "d," and "the backseat of a BMW"
came to mind, read on.

Chastity imposes awkward restrictions on courtship, but they are far less awkward than conceiving a new little person or contracting a terminal disease. A randy young priglet who yearns to remain pure will benefit greatly from chanting "Condoms break" like a mantra until his or her wedding night. Heterosexual men who wish to curb their lust may wish to screen the recent movies of Elizabeth Taylor (monitoring her multiple chins) or study the vast expanses of naked, unshaven female flesh that illustrate the first edition of *Our Bodies, Ourselves*. The novels of Erica Jong are also an effective anti-aphrodisiac, as is the homoerotic poetry of Allen Ginsberg. There is, however, a downside to the latter method: if you come to regard your mouth as a receptacle for sick-making bodily secretions, you could become anorexic.

Whenever possible, neo-prigs should try to date one another. Intermarriage can sometimes work, but inter-courtship is by definition impossible. If you are a male non-prig and you attempt to woo a female prig, she'll have you arrested for date rape the second or third time you go out. Likewise, if you are a female non-prig and you attempt to woo a male prig, you had better be prepared to achieve sexual satisfaction by yourself.

Where Can I Meet Other Prigs?

If you are an ordained minister, a federal prosecutor, or an IRS agent, it will be easy for you to meet other prigs among your colleagues. If, however, you are a cocktail waitress or an executive with Philip Morris, meeting new prigs will be harder.

To meet like-minded people, many neo-prigs take up hobbies. If you like small, cuddly beasts and are willing to chuck your ancient raccoon coat, you might want to become involved in the animal rights movement. And if you are a male prig who is excessively fond of other male prigs, join Aesthetic Realism. Other surefire places to meet prigs include the Vatican, Salt Lake City, St. Bartholemew's, and England.

Where Should One Take a Prig on a Date?

Some prig dates happen spontaneously: going out for decaf after an AA meeting, spotting for one another while you lift weights at the gym, sitting in adjacent seats at an Evelyn Wood Reading Dynamics course or some other self-improvement seminar.

But when a neo-prig catches another neo-prig's eye—and the thought of marriage looms in the distant but not unforeseeable future—the two of them will eventually have to go out on a formal date.

The tone of a couple's first hours together sets the tone of their relationship. Consequently, some prigs I know like to have an elderly aunt accompany them as a chaperone. If, however, all your elderly aunts tend to engage strangers in discussions of the "postmenopausal orgasm," you might want to invite a nun.

Regardless of whether or not you go out with a chaperone, your destination should not be chosen casually. Museums are too risqué—full of lurid Old Master nudes and contemporary sadomasochistic photography. Maybe for the second or third date, but they provide the wrong ambience for your first time together.

A Broadway play is also a bad idea—particularly if it was written by Lanford Wilson, Sam Shepherd or David Mamet. These usually amount to little more than foul-mouthed actors yelling "f-ck" at one another. And as for ballet, those firm young bodies in tight costumes can't help but bring unclean thoughts to mind. Opera, too, is out of the question. The plots are often sympathetic to unsavory characters: Violetta in *La Traviata* is a prostitute, the Marschallin in *Der Rosenkavalier* is an adulteress, as is the eponymous Carmen. Then there are the incestuous adulterers Siegmund and Sieglinde in *Die Walküre*. Goodness, the list is long.

Even something as ostensibly innocent as a stroll in the park is fraught with dangers: filthy verses of rap music pouring out of some suitcase-sized stereo, a glimpse of two male non-prigs copulating in the bushes, even (if the stroll occurs at dusk) the prospect of being gang-raped and murdered.

After extended interviews with hundreds of ardent neo-prigs, however, several preferred destinations emerged:

1. a revival of *The Sound of Music*

2. the Ice Capades

3. church

"Let me take you to paradise" can be an appropriate prig come-on if the speaker advocates the ecclesiastically sanctioned path: a blameless life and holy death.

Non-Prig Date	Prig Date
Jungle-green piña coladas and sweet-and-sour pork at Trader Vic's	Water and brown rice at the Dali Lama Macrobiotic Kitchen
The new Mamet play on Broadway	*Holiday on Ice*
More piña coladas and dancing at the Paradise Garage	Unsweetened lemondade at Rumpelmayer's
Home to his king-size Simmons mattress after a brief, athletic stint on the Berber carpet just inside the front door	Home by midnight to their respective monastic cots

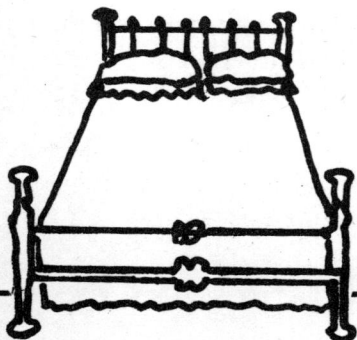

Getting Serious

Non-prig couples can express romantic interest in a variety of ways, usually involving mutual pawing and the removal of clothes. Frequently, if they wish to precipitate coronaries in their parents, they will move in together. Prigs, however, do not have these options. A dry, chaste kiss and an exchange of jewelry—not (shudder) saliva—is about as far as they can go.

Prigs who are seriously hot for one another should arrange to visit only by letter, telephone, or fax. If seclusion doesn't diminish their feeling, they will know they have found the "real thing." And they will be ready to enter the grandest commitment of their neo-prig lives: the covenant of marriage.

How to Pop the Question

In traditional prig culture, a man is expected to request his beloved's hand in marriage—often not from the woman herself but from her father. Neo-prigs, by contrast, are more flexible. If a woman's biological clock is ticking loudly enough, she herself may pop the fateful question. And these days men know far too much about both feminism and biology to petition their loved one's father for any part of their beloved—most especially her "hand."

What Do I Do
If My Beloved Says No?

There are three approaches:

*1. Tell them they are selfish, shallow,
desicated cretins and they are
destined to spend the rest of their lives
shriveling in solitude.
2. Beg them.
3. Weep profusely and beg them.*

What Do I Do
If My Beloved Says Yes?

Offer a prayer of thanksgiving.

*If you are female, expect to receive
a small, discreet diamond.*

*If you are male, expect to receive
(from the bride's parents) a small, discreet
wedding ceremony. And phone your
lawyer to get cracking on a
prenuptial agreement.*

J. Edgar Hoover

In an effort to deflate the mystique surrounding certain big-time gangsters in the 30s, J. Edgar Hoover, "Mr. FBI" for over half a century, worked to glamorize the exploits of federal agents Eliot Ness and the "Untouchables." In later years, however, Hoover became obsessed with recording other exploits—notably the checkered sex lives of Dr. Martin Luther King, Jr., and the late Kennedy brothers.

Cardinal John O'Connor

From the pulpit of Manhattan's St. Patrick's Cathedral, this valiant crusader has ceaselessly fought the evils of abortion, homosexuality, rock music, and condoms. With absolutely no sense of public relations, he has embraced controversy— and, with the possible exception of Torquemada, generated more anti-Catholic sentiment than any cleric in recorded history.

The
National
Celibacy
Corps

Editor's note: This chapter is meant to shed some light on the mysterious "National Celibacy Corps" which has been convening since the late 1980s in church basements and student unions and community centers across America. But despite the enormous popularity of this group, it's not right for everyone. Many fine young prigs are blessed with absolutely no sex drive whatsoever, and however laudable they may find the goals of the NCC, it's not a place they will feel at home.

What Is the National Celibacy Corps?

A support group and recovery program for unmarried women (and men) who want to overcome their addiction to s-x.

How Does the NCC Work?

Local chapters meet at least weekly and sometimes daily in nearly every American city and in many cities throughout the world. A typical meeting begins with introductions—first name only—to ensure members' privacy. Veterans and novices alike are encouraged to stand up and say, "My name is X and I am impure," then to share their temptations—and discuss why they succumbed or how they resisted. Meetings end with a recitation of the "Five Steps" and the NCC pledge.

New members are asked to select a "partner" of the same gender whom they can call at any hour of the day or night if they find themselves tempted by sexual passion. This partner agrees to counsel them, visit them, and do everything short of physical violence to keep them away from sin. They, in turn, agree to do the same for their partner.

Members also study techniques to diminish sexual arousal in their loved ones. These include feigning attacks of asthma, food poisoning, and epilepsy. Female members

are encouraged to carry a Swiss Army knife while on dates and, if provoked, shout, "Don't think I won't cut it off." Loved ones who find these techniques erotic should be dropped instantly.

The NCC is not a magic formula, a quick fix, or an instant answer. It is a process—long-term and at times frustrating. And often it works too well: members contemplating marriage are encouraged to spend at least two months debriefing before they attempt to consummate their union.

What Are the Five Steps?

1. We admit that we are powerless over s-x — that our lives have become unmanageable.

2. We believe that a Power greater than ourselves can restore us to chastity.

3. We have decided to turn our will and our lives away from the pleasures of the flesh.

4. We have made a list of all the persons we have lusted after, and whenever possible, we make amends to them.

5. We have tried to carry this message to all unmarried people, and to practice these principles in all our affairs.

When I Meet a New Person, How Can I Tell If He or She Is a Member?

The NCC has a number of slogans—many of which are emblazoned on buttons, T-shirts, and lapel pins. They include *Trust not lust*, *One night at a time*, and *God is my roommate*.

Male members disinclined to wear message clothing are nearly impossible to identify, but female members can be detected by the large red stop sign on the ceiling above their beds . . .

STOP
IF HE KNOCKS YOU UP,
HE CAN TAKE YOUR PLACE
AT HARVARD LAW SCHOOL.

Members also carry a wallet-sized card containing the NCC pledge.

NCC PLEDGE

On my honor, I will try to resist temptation at all times, to support my sisters and brothers who share this goal, and to avoid fraternity parties, crack houses, and deserted beaches from now until the hour of my marriage.

_____

Signature

How Did the NCC Begin?

Somewhere in the Midwest, circa 1988: it had been a rough night at the Psi Iota Gamma fraternity house. As the sun rose over a campus that shall remain unnamed, Barbie C. and Suzy S.—members of PIG's sister sorority—were emerging from comas in a downstairs recreation room. Above them was a chart—detailing the ounces of grain alcohol required to lead certain malleable coeds into bed.

As Barbie and Suzy regained consciousness, rummaged for their clothes, and checked themselves into the university rape crisis center, it dawned on them that being "popular" was not all it was cracked up to be. And as they attempted unsuccessfully to prosecute their assailants, they realized that the double standard was back: young men who fooled around risked virtually nothing; young women, by contrast, risked everything.

Because the girls were far too heterosexual for another alternative to suggest itself to them, they came to a bold conclusion: women—particularly young women—must simply band together and renounce sex.

Barbie and Suzy knew it would not be easy. They knew men and women alike would receive their message with scorn. But because they had personally suffered the perils of promiscuity, they couldn't keep their message to themselves.

The first NCC meeting took place in Suzy's apartment. Present were Barbie, Suzy, Suzy's Yorkshire terrier, and the three friends who still talked to them. The next week Suzy placed an ad in the campus newspaper. Several undergraduates, a faculty child, and an unmarried female professor of Russian literature showed up. Within months, their little group had doubled. And to their surprise, a quarter of the new members were men.

Yes, as Barbie and Suzy learned, men suffered from promiscuity, too. They were afraid of diseases, afraid of impotence, and afraid that if they didn't f-ck all the time, "the guys" would brand them homosexuals. NCC meetings were a breath of fresh air: they could meet girls and get to know them instead of being compelled to "perform."

Word soon spread to other campuses. New groups were formed. And today the NCC has chapters at nearly every college in America.

How Can I Join?

Check your telephone directory for the number of the nearest chapter of the NCC. Or if you know a member personally, ask if you may accompany him or her to a meeting. The NCC welcomes members of all races, colors, affectional preferences, and creeds.

Savonarola

Savonarola, the notorious Florentine religious reformer whose career ended in martyrdom, was the instigator of the original "Bonfire of the Vanities"—a public burning in 1497 of lewd pictures, cards, and gaming tables. If Fra Bartolommeo's famous portrait of him is at all accurate, Savonarola was not, shall we say, a looker. This may provide some insight into his mad pursuit of moral purity: the poor fellow never had any opportunities to stray.

Don Johnson and Melanie Griffith (After the Remarriage)

These two adorable kids first fell for one another when he was 22 and she a mere 14. Four years later, they married, divorced, and followed separate but remarkably similar paths: drug addiction, alcohol abuse, and B movies. Last year, however, with Griffith's career (instead of Griffith) on a high, the two remarried—and now live happily ever after in Aspen, Beverly Hills, and Miami, with their new daughter, Dakota Mayi. (By the time this book sees print, however, who knows, who knows?)

Hugh Hefner
(After the Marriage)

Once the crown prince of porn, Hugh Hefner is now married. Henpecked, even: his bride has given birth, his grown-up daughter is running what little remains of his empire, and, according to the *National Enquirer*, his mother-in-law has moved into the Playboy Mansion. Can anyone doubt we've entered the Decade of the Prig?

The Prig Wedding

In the old days, before the advent of neo-prudery, champagne flowed freely at wedding receptions. Guests were expected to get a little tipsy—to dance and flirt and devour six courses of undistinguished banquet food, after which the groom's boozy Aunt Ida would blurt out family secrets and at least two strangers who had only just met would wander off together to exchange bodily fluids.

Today, however, no right-thinking person would tolerate such a squalid scenario. Marriage, after all, is a Serious Commitment—not, perhaps, as serious as one's career, but not something to be taken lightly.

Consequently, no prig couple would dream of staging a wedding for the benefit of their friends and family. The ideal wedding is a tax-deductible social gathering—spar-

kling with celebrities and high-ranking professional colleagues. A few friends and socially presentable relatives may
be present, but not many. And if (through some misguided
burst of sentimentality) the groom invites boozy Aunt Ida,
he should hire a bodyguard to keep her off both the hooch
and the bride's Uncle Pete.

The formula for the perfect prig wedding is simple: if
any aspect of it sounds like fun, you're doing something
wrong. And of course—with both of your careers on the
line—you wouldn't want to do that.

Should I Announce My Wedding in the Newspaper?

Without question. Because it is tacky, vulgar, and not
professionally useful to sneak off and get married, this step
is a must. There is, however, a right and wrong way to go
about it.

Study the following two texts and determine which
version is preferred:

Text A:

Heidi Burger Lovejoy, a daughter of Mr. and Mrs. Walter Haynes Lovejoy of Darien, Connecticut, was married yesterday to John Sherman Warshawski, a son of Mr. Wilbur "Shifty" Warshawski of Leavenworth, Kansas, and Mrs. Virgil Snopes of Reno, Nevada. Judge Henry Fowler officiated at the Brazen Lobster Restaurant in New York City.

The bride, an account executive at the advertising agency of Fain and Blote, is a graduate of Vassar College. Her father is a partner in the investment firm of Gelt, Gelt and Luker. Her mother, Louise Lovejoy, teaches beginning and intermediate fox trot at Ginger Rogers Community College.

The bridegroom, a graduate of East Delaware State College, is a science writer for Tabloid Today. *His first two marriages ended in divorce. His father is a license-plate manufacturing engineer and his mother, Rita May Snopes, is the president of the Western Regional Elvis Presley We-Know-You-Are-Alive Association.*

Text B:

Heidi Burger Lovejoy, daughter of Mr. and Mrs. Walter Haynes Lovejoy of Darien, Connecticut, was married yesterday to John Sherman Smith, an orphan. Reverend Alfred Evensong performed the ceremony at the All Saints' Episcopal Church in New Canaan, Connecticut.

The bride, an account executive at the advertising agency of Fain and Blote, is a graduate of Vassar College. Her father is a partner in the investment firm of Gelt, Gelt and Luker. Her mother, Louise Lovejoy, is a teacher.

The bridegroom, a graduate of Harvard College, is the science writer for Tabloid Today.

If you found text "B" preferable, go on to "The Bridal Shower." If, however, you found nothing wrong with "A," keep reading.

Incarcerated parents, former spouses, and second-rate colleges have no place in your wedding announcement! Never let accuracy interfere with good taste. If, however, you insist on being honest, volunteer a minimum of information and cast it in the best light possible. Don't, for instance, refer to Mr. Warshawski as "a" science writer, make him "the" science writer. Better yet, refer to him as Mr. Smith: not only does it sound better, it permits you to invent his alma mater. As any fact checker will tell you, lots of Mr. Smiths (and not many Mr. Warshawskis) graduate from good colleges every year.

Finally, under no circumstances permit a judge to marry you. Prigs are a God-fearing people, whether or not they believe in Him. Judges exist to marry Commies and atheists—you go find yourself a clergyman.

Wedding Picture Dos and Don'ts:

RIGHT

One more thing: if you expect the newspaper to run a photograph with your announcement, present them with a suitable image. Check your phone book for photographers who specialize in this field (you might try under "A" for "airbrush") and make sure to arrive at your photo session with at least three of the following: a pearl necklace, ash-blonde hair, a tortoiseshell hairband, pearl earrings, clear blue eyes, a retroussé nose, dimples, a bow-shaped mouth, and prominent white teeth.

WRONG

The Bridal Shower

Guidelines for this event are more flexible than you might think. I have, for example, known the prissiest of female prigs to squeal with delight at "lingerie showers"— as long as it is clearly stipulated on the invitation that all garments presented to the bride must be white, must be made from natural fibers, and must not have been purchased from Frederick's of Hollywood. Also, any garment the bride might not know how to use should come with a set of instructions. And as for the appropriate food and beverages, anything goes—anything without alcohol, that is.

The Bachelor Party

Unless the best man (who traditionally organizes this event) can persuade the groom's friends to make a retreat at a Carthusian or Cistercian monastery, avoid it. Traditional bachelor parties are, alas, nearly always occasions of sin.

Where to Get Married

Traditional prigs and neo-prigs are divided on this issue. Traditional prigs have a sentimental attachment to home—particularly when home is Winesburg, Ohio, Fond du Lac, Wisconsin, or Tyler, Texas—and are willing to sacrifice a power wedding for that small-town *je ne sais quoi*.

Neo-prigs, by contrast, have too much vested in their social mountaineering to return to the backwaters whence they derived. Consequently, they prefer to celebrate their marriages in the New Yorks and Washingtons—the Londons and Saint-Moritzes—the Sodoms and Gomorrahs—where they currently reside.

Often this poses daunting challenges for neo-prigs. Except for a few isolated enclaves in Pasadena, for example, there is nearly nowhere in Los Angeles where a prig marriage can be performed tastefully. But even if you can't be married under ideal circumstances, certain spots are so patently vulgar as to be unthinkable. These include:

1. Malibu at dawn

2. Waikiki at dawn

3. The Grand Canyon at dawn

4. The boardwalk in Atlantic City any time of day

5. Anywhere in Las Vegas—or Nevada, for that matter

6. Greenwich Village—unless it is 1906, you are Edith Newbold Jones, and you are about to marry Teddy Wharton in Grace Church

7. City Hall—better to be married by a Moonie or a Krishna than to defile a sacred institution by exchanging secular vows

What Should I Wear?

For her: white, white, and more white. Many female prigs favor long dresses with sleeves—but sleeves are essential only if your biceps are adorned with needle tracks or problematic tattoos. And go easy on the makeup—this is the *last* time in your life you'd want to resemble a painted woman.

For him: black, black, and more black. The notion of a dinner jacket in a color appropriate to a breath mint or a baby blanket is too revolting to contemplate. Moreover, ruffles have not been acceptable on shirts since the eighteenth century.

The Reception

What Should I Serve?

The perfect prig wedding is dry. Because, however, some older guests (fossils in their fifties) may be alcohol-addicted, it's wise to make a small amount of wine available to them. Withdrawal symptoms—which may involve the withdrawal of expensive wedding gifts—are not attractive.

For the healthy younger crowd, you'll want to have a deluxe, fully stocked water bar—featuring 100 percent natural mineral elixirs from around the world. Among the must-serves are Poland Spring, Saratoga Spring, and Apollinaris water, not to mention lots of Ramlösa in those exquisite crystal-blue bottles. Factory-flavored waters and waters in (shudder) plastic bottles are, however, taboo.

Even for traditional prigs, the days of six-course sit-down dinners are long gone. Nonetheless, traditional prigs like their wedding fare to evoke memories of childhood, of the innocence they are on the cusp of losing: Ritz crackers, pigs-in-a-blanket, Cheez Whiz. And something substantial—say, prime rib, canned asparagus, baked potatoes inlaid with chives—for the buffet.

Urban neo-prigs, however, resist culinary nostalgia. They will want to serve the same affected things at their wedding that they learned to love at their favorite overpriced restaurants: blackened quail legs on a bed of peeled grapes; baby carrots so tiny as to be almost unborn; macrobiotic rice—anything as long as you can't taste it and it doesn't diminish your hunger.

Should I Hire a Band?

Except for one week of noise twenty years ago at Woodstock, live music has always been preferable to the canned variety. Harpists and string quartets are perfect for weddings, conjuring up as they do childhood images of winged choirs on high. And although dancing is inspired by the devil, it has long been traditional at wedding receptions. Consequently, employing a dance band is permissible—as long as their repertory doesn't include those filthy ditties you endure in aerobics class.

What Flowers Should I Buy?

Wedding flowers should be small, white, and unobtrusive. Anthuriums, with their lewd pistils waving in the air, are more suitable for a brothel than a betrothal—as is any flower ever painted by Georgia O'Keeffe. Avoid arrangements that look like this:

How Do I Know If the Reception Was a Success?

If a prig wedding is pulled off properly, it will be possible for everyone—especially the bride and groom—to momentarily forget that when the guests leave, they will be expected to go off and acquire carnal knowledge of one another.

Margaret Thatcher

In the 1980s, this grocer's daughter and English prime minister single-handedly revitalized a nation of shiftless white people. Many observers feel her finest hours occurred during the Falklands crisis—in which she enlisted all the resources of Her Majesty's Navy to protect a sheep-infested rock on the other side of the world from a saber-rattling banana republic.

Doris Day

To anyone who cares about Truth, Beauty, Motherhood and wholesome entertainment, it should come as no surprise that once—in 1967—Doris Day was the world's number-one box office star. But as films grew artier (read: more squalid) and romantic comedies gave way to orgiastic romps, the freckle-faced, ever-virgin actress was relegated to the Love Canal of oblivion, where, except for a few forays to the White House to champion animal rights, her new pet cause, she remains today.

How to Make Love to a Prig

In at least one respect, prigs are just like you and me: in order to make babies, they still have to insert the same body parts into the same places.

People who haven't been putting those body parts in those places regularly, however, will have more trouble with the process than those who have. Consequently, prigs should embark on their voyage of carnal discovery with a *Honeymoon Survival Kit:*

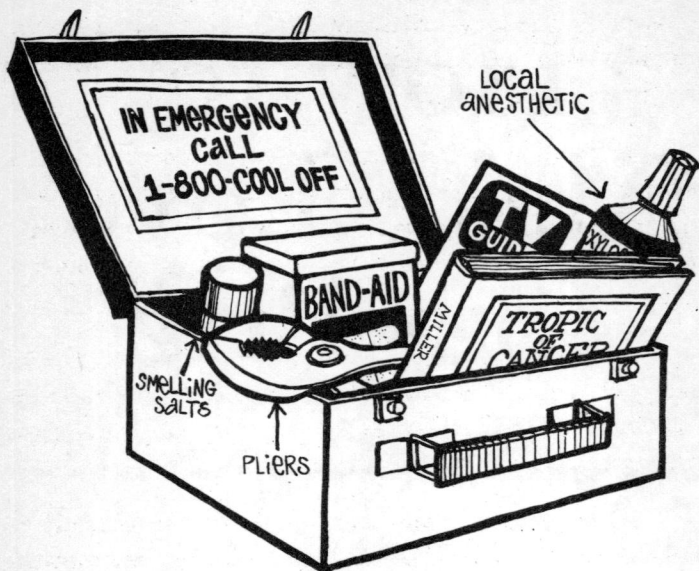

It also contains these helpful hints:

1. If you are a man and your you-know-what has found its way into a pleasant, untraditional orifice, remove it immediately. Otherwise, you will burn in hell forever.

2. If you are a woman and you feel anything but extreme discomfort while making love, something is wrong. Heed the words of Evelyn Waugh: "All this fuss about sleeping together. For physical pleasure I'd sooner go to my dentist any day."

3. If while having sex you ever find yourself thinking of other partners—particularly those of the same sex or animals—stop immediately, kneel at the side of the bed, and pray for forgiveness.

4. If you're too tense to make love without a few belts of Scotch or a few puffs of marijuana, sneak off and consume them in private. If you don't, your prig partner will remind you of the disastrous effect those substances have on fertility.

5. Don't even think about smoking in bed. I know of one prig who overturned an aquarium on her lover and his cigarette after he bequeathed to her what he is certain was the first and only orgasm of her life.

6. If you are female and you find it exciting to have your breasts pawed and sucked upon, make an appointment with a psychiatrist. You are a very sick person. For a socially acceptable version of those thrills, see the chapter on the prig way of birth.

7. If your partner whispers unprintable four-letter words—or even words like "hot" or "baby" that are printable in other contexts—threaten to divorce him or her. Alternatively, keep a bar of Ivory soap by the bed and insert it in his or her offending mouth.

8. If you are female and your partner buys you the sort of underwear appropriate for a hooker, don't wear it. And don't let him wear it either!

9. If you are a male, keep your socks on at all times while making love.

10. Scrub thoroughly with a reliable antiseptic before and after sex. And don't forget to brush and floss.

11. Should you find it necessary to cry out in the throes of passion, do not take the name of the Lord in vain.

12. Flannel is a prig aphrodisiac. Whenever possible, wear flannel pajamas or nightdresses—even if it means setting your air conditioner at "super cool."

13. Finally, keep a change of linens near the marital bed. Prigs do not sleep on wet spots.

If one of you is a non-prig, it's essential to memorize these suggestions. They'll keep you from offending (or injuring) your partner.

And if both of you are prigs, take heart: once you've managed to conceive a child, outsiders will cease to judge you. They won't care whether or not you ever do the horrible deed again. You can even tiptoe off to an occasional National Celibacy Corps meeting, if you yearn for your old way of life.

The Prig Way of Birth

If you're a married female prig, you can achieve nine months of paradise simply by becoming pregnant. Think of it: no more pressure to guzzle Heineken or stay up late. No more pressure to drink coffee! Even non-prigs are concerned about birth defects: they will smile with approval as you wolf down multiple vitamins, spinach, prunes, nonfat milk—all the wholesome things that non-prigs despise and you, naturally, adore. What's more, if a non-prig lights a cigarette near you, you can screech at him to put it out and he will shrug apologetically and comply.

If you're not by nature a prig, however, motherhood will transform you into one. Not only will you cease to

crave caffeine and alcohol, they will make you violently ill. Likewise—for the first three months or so—will some meat products and spicy foods. Never in your life will assimilation into prig culture come so easily.

There is one catch: you must retain your innocence. It's fine to know all there is to know about prenatal nutrition and fetal development, but you must feign ignorance of the act that got you knocked up in the first place. This is the litmus test: can you while severely pregnant argue with conviction that the stork brings babies?

If you insist on being biologically accurate, however, make it clear to prigs that procreative sex is no fun. Talk about the nuisance of taking your temperature each morning to determine when you are ovulating. Make your sexual encounters sound as distasteful and strenuous as preparing for an IRS audit.

For non-prigs, infertility problems are a curse, a source of shame and depression. Prigs, however, delight in the struggle. Many actually prefer to have their child conceived in a petri dish: the process is tidy, asexual, and something only the relatively rich can afford.

Prig motherhood desexualizes your body. You need no longer be inhibited about exposing parts of it. Study the behavior of prig mothers—they're as unself-consciously exhibitionistic as aerobics instructors. Woman who before they gave birth would no more dream of exposing their knees to sunlight suddenly whip out their breasts in public and attach little Junior. Likewise women too prim to reveal their navels on the beach pass around Polaroids of themselves in the delivery room, legs splayed, discharging their offspring.

Prig mothers enjoy making other mothers feel inferior. If you confess to a prig mom that you had a few drinks before you found out you were pregnant, she'll deliver a long lecture about fetal alcohol syndrome. And should you express difficulty in eating enough protein each day without gaining a lot of weight, she'll talk about how she didn't have to change her diet when she became pregnant: she ate healthy food all along.

Prig mothers are the first to show up at Lamaze class and the last to leave. They are self-righteous about the use of drugs during childbirth—they never took them before and they don't intend to start taking them now. Extremist prigs even balk at epidurals—the trendy anesthesia that permits people with normal thresholds of pain to remain more or less alert while expelling their offspring. These prigs want to give birth "naturally."

Ironically, when push—so to speak—comes to shove, many prigs wind up having Caesareans. If you wake up in the maternity ward next to a prig recovering from abdominal surgery, try not to say, "I told you so." Try not to point out that because you took drugs and were in less pain you didn't require that drastic measure. The shock, the humiliation, and the sense of failure are already more punishment than the average prig can bear.

Here are a few guidelines to help you become a prissier parent:

1. If you worry about the pain of childbirth, don't bare your soul to any pregnant neo-prigs. They will make you feel unworthy of the institution of motherhood.

2. Spend a great deal of money on pin-striped, dress-for-success maternity clothes. You are a having-it-all power mother—and you don't want your secretarial underlings to forget it.

3. Learn what birth defects obscure substances like quinine can cause. Then describe them to other pregnant mothers while they are sipping their quinine-laden lime tonics.

4. If you're a male neo-prig and your wife is expecting, practice with your video camera to ensure that every second of her beautiful birth experience is recorded for other neo-prig couples to enjoy.

5. Do hire an upright, corn-fed Midwestern farm girl as a nanny for your children. Don't import a lazy, tarty French au pair who will make goo-goo eyes at Daddy instead of at his offspring. If you insist on a European au pair, employ an East German *Fräulein*, preferably Prussian, who has been taking steroids as part of her *Freie Deutsche Jugend* after-school athletic program. At least she can be counted upon to discipline the kids.

6. Don't use disposable diapers. Sure, cloth diapers are a nuisance, but think of the pleasure you'll get accusing parents who buy Pampers—which are not biodegradable—that they are raping the environment.

7. Don't bottle-feed. Sneer at mothers who do so. Anything that convenient can't possibly be good for a child.

8. And finally, don't believe all that liberal claptrap about letting your child learn to use the toilet when he or she feels like it. Toilet-training must be approached with quasi-fascist intensity. Like charity, anal-compulsiveness begins at home.

How to Raise a Perfect Prig

If you were conscientious about prenatal nutrition, you should have produced a beautiful, brilliant, perfectly adjusted child. If, on the other hand, you had a drop of wine or pinch of sugar, you could be in for big trouble.

Prig children are not like other children. They play only with tasteful Beatrix Potter stuffed animals, not with vulgar, colorful Garfield toys. They never soil (or even rumple) their Laura Ashley pinafores or break their impeccable porcelain mugs. Nor do they apply red Magic Marker to their bedroom wallpaper or toss their hand-painted wooden alphabet blocks through windows.

This is because they're usually manacled—to a Third World servant who has been instructed, under threat of discharge, not to permit them to behave childishly. Some Third World servants, however, are untrustworthy: they sneak the children plastic mugs and lurid toys—Barbie dolls, Smurfs, and simulated assault weapons—when you're not around.

Children brought up in prig households don't discover chocolate, Coca-Cola, or television until they start kindergarten. They don't discover words like *f-ck* until they start college. And they don't actually perform the activity that word refers to until well after they are married.

Diet

Because hyperactivity has been linked to the excessive consumption of sweets, a prig parent has a moral imperative to be a Nutrition Nazi. All sweets should be banished from a household where there are children under twelve. If that seems too drastic, at least bear these things in mind:

- The best way to ensure that your child doesn't develop a taste for ice cream is to prevent him or her from ever sampling it.

- Children will love beets and turnips and Brussels sprouts if these items are their only means of obtaining nutrition.

- Egg whites and tofu will seem downright "nummy" to children who have never tasted a bacon cheeseburger.

- And never, ever permit your child to sample sugar-coated vitamins in the shape of cartoon characters: the experience could undermine irrevocably all of your teachings on the dangers of sugar.

Kiddie cholesterol problems are the dark side of permissive child-rearing. As a parent, it's your role to guide your child onto the path of dietary righteousness before he or she reaches the age of seven.

Self-Abuse

It is also your role to imbue your son or daughter with a reverence for chastity. If your children ask where they came from, tell them, "Mount Sinai Hospital." If they persist, tell them they were found in a cabbage patch. Don't, under any circumstances, construct stories about Daddy's "seed" in Mommy's "tummy"; the little monsters will demand to know how it got there.

If your little one's hands roam toward his or her unmentionable places at night, you will want to acquire a Victorian Decency Device. This handy set of gadgets—available in surgical steel—attach to any crib or playpen.

If, however, your offspring's mitts venture there during church services or in front of your extremely proper and undoubtedly frigid Aunt Edna, you should beat your child one hundred times with a briar cane. This may cause psychological problems later—but that is far better than causing you embarrassment now. And besides, there's always

the possibility that it won't cause any damage. Some of the most robust prigs I know were beaten as children.

Education

In Japan, where university admission is highly competitive, some students who don't make the grade commit suicide every year. In America, when a student fails, it's far more likely that the parents will commit suicide.

Neo-prigs, in particular, place education first. They want their child to have every opportunity, right from the moment of conception. Some expectant mothers have been known to play audiotapes of conversational French within earshot of their protruding abdomens. Others begin their child's reading instruction in English at six months old; in Latin, at a year and a half. And nearly all enroll their child in a competitive, Harvard-track preschool by the age of two.

Prig children learn early to handle stress. No matter how harried and pressured their adult lives become, they will never again have to cram eight academic courses, ballet lessons, piano lessons, tennis lessons, riding lessons, skating lessons, art lessons, and dancing school into a mere seven-day week.

Prigs who live in affluent suburban neighborhoods with high property taxes often send their children to the local public school. They're paying dearly for it, they figure, so why not? Prig children in this environment are easy to spot. At the urging of their parents, they perform the ultimate

My Day

by Constance Priglet, age 9

8: French tutor
9: School
10:
11:
12:
1:
2:
3: Ballet class
4: Karate class / junior aerobics
5: Quality time with Mummy
6: Dinner
7: Homework (No television. Ever.)
8: Quality time with Daddy (if slow night at office)
8:30 Bedtime prayers
8:45 Lights Out

report card
A

self-portrait

job for prigs-in-training: hall monitor. This job teaches them not only to rat on their peers but also to snoop, ferret out wrongdoing, and condescend to offenders—skills that will serve them well in adulthood.

For the most part, however, neo-prigs send their off-spring away to boarding school. This is because it's easier to gain admission to a "good" college if they've distinguished themselves at a good preparatory school. And even if they've underachieved, they're more likely to get in if they demonstrate that Mom and Dad can afford to pay. Another advantage of boarding school: If your fourteen-year-old delights in heavy metal music, at least you don't have to listen to it.

Traditional prigs and neo-prigs are at odds about where to go to college. Traditional prigs believe that a good religious background and stern discipline can compensate for an undistinguished academic program. Neo-prigs demand that their sons and daughters matriculate with the best and the brightest. They sneer at offbeat, funky colleges like Antioch, Oberlin, and the University of California at Santa Cruz, and withhold tuition if their child is accepted there. And if they're proud alumni, they threaten to disinherit children who don't at least *apply* to their alma maters.

There is one thing that all varieties of prig agree upon, however: reputable young men and women do not attend "party" schools. If during spring break more than half of a school's student body uproots itself to Fort Lauderdale to guzzle beer and throw Frisbees, that school is inappropriate for prigs.

These colleges are most popular with traditional prigs:

- Bob Jones University—because no matter what the Constitution says, miscegenation is still a terrible idea.

- Bethany Nazarene Bible College—because many fine, upstanding men and women—as well as Gary Hart— passed through its portals.

- Brigham Young University—because it's filled with wholesome young Mormons who drink neither coffee nor alcohol and (these days) believe in monogamy.

Neo-prig favorites include:

- Harvard University—because of that Puritan *je ne sais quoi.*

- California Institute of Technology—because plastic pocket protectors are part of the mandatory dress code.

- University of Notre Dame—just because.

Certain colleges, however, are grossly unacceptable to both traditional and neo-prigs. They include:

- Yale University—because it has graduate schools in drama, music, and art—and you know what kind of people *they* attract.

- Dartmouth College—because prigs are not "animals."

- Bennington College—because it is an incubator for new strains of sexually transmitted diseases. (If you don't believe this, read the novels of Bret Easton Ellis.)

The vast majority of American colleges fall somewhere between the perfect and the unthinkable. Most smart young prigs should have no trouble finding an environment that is right for them: where they will be—insofar as a prig can be—happy.

Rudolph Giuliani

From his crusade against insider traders to his unsuccessful court battle against aging beauty queen Bess Myerson and her mob-connected, sewer-contractor beau, Andy Capasso, Rudy Giuliani has been a federal prosecutor who garnered headlines. Unfortunately, headlines were not enough to garner him votes: last year, the saintlier-than-thou Republican lost New York City's mayoral race to old-time back-room pol and Democrat David Dinkins.

Choosing
a Career

Prigs, for the most part, make excellent bureaucrats. They are at home in large corporations and are fiercely loyal to people in authority. They are not likely to join labor unions or go on strike—except occasionally to spy on behalf of management. Prigs live to work for firms like IBM, and are a very good risk when it comes to hiring. They rarely defect to other corporations and never venture into business for themselves.

Prigs also do well in the ecclesiastical hierarchy. Many bishops, archbishops, cardinals, and, yes, even popes have been prigs. Religious prigs who like to go camping often go into missionary work. Missionary prigs, however, are more likely to be slaughtered and devoured by indigenous peoples than they are to assist revolutionaries in constructing bombs.

Prigs who go into law rarely become public defenders. They occasionally join corporate firms, but the vast majority of them become prosecutors. Prigs are particularly well-suited to inquisitions. And, of course, there exists an entire federal agency staffed entirely by former hall monitors: the Internal Revenue Service.

While very few prigs enjoy the legwork involved in newspaper reporting, they make excellent copy editors. Prigs usually spell well and know every conceivable obscure rule of grammar. They delight in transforming graceful prose into a stilted, unreadable, perfectly grammatical mess that sounds as if a computer had composed it. They love telling reporters that some minor fact in a story they wrote is "Wrong, wrong, wrong!" This is not, however, to say that prigs make excellent *editors*. Editors also assign stories and design pages, chores which require imagination, a rare commodity among the priggish.

Prigs in the medical profession usually become dentists or surgeons. They're obsessed with flossing, plaque removal, incipient gingivitis, and the deleterious effects of inadequate brushing. To them, the charm of surgery is the sterility of the operating room. Prigs love scrubbing with antiseptic, wearing germ-proof masks, and working with pristine, autoclaved instruments. These days, many prigs also choose obstetrics—for the thrill of orchestrating drug-free deliveries.

About the only specialty prig doctors avoid is psychiatry, particularly psychoanalysis. If prigs deny the existence of sex, they're certainly not going to sit for hours listening to a crazy person who wants nothing more than to talk about it.

Although I know a handful of writers, two architects, and at least one musician who are prigs, for the most part, prigs tend not to gravitate into the arts. This is especially true in fields such as painting or sculpture, where it's nearly impossible to work without getting your hands dirty. And despite their fondness for aerobics, prigs lack the sensuality to become great dancers.

When in doubt about choosing a career, would-be prigs should follow this simple rule: anything requiring creativity, talent, and imagination is to be avoided.

Anita Bryant

This former Florida orange juice promoter, wife, and mother risked her booming singing career for what she considered to be her God-given mission: an anti-homosexual "Save the Children" campaign. Although her crusade appeared to have had little impact on either gay people or children, it did destroy orange juice sales in a nationwide boycott and led to her dismissal as a spokesperson for the product.

Prig Utopia

Where do prigs prefer to live?

a. Outside a 100-mile radius of Manhattan

b. Inside a 100-mile radius of Disneyworld (not Disneyland – it's too close to Los Angeles)

c. Near their jobs

d. All of the above [correct answer]

There was a time when prigs resided in suburban houses with tailored lawns, white picket fences, and basements that had been converted into fallout shelters. Ideally, these houses were in alcohol-free counties which had, at most, a single movie theater. Video stores, with their myriad evils,

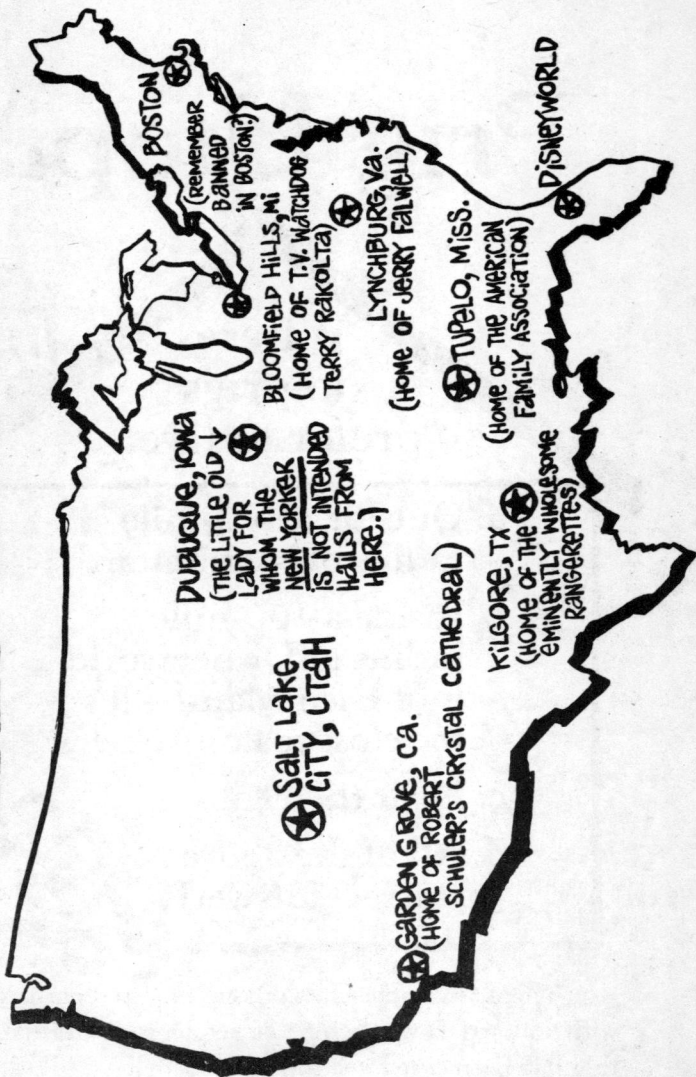

PRIG AMERICA

BOSTON
(REMEMBER
BANNED
IN BOSTON?)

BLOOMFIELD HILLS, MI
(HOME OF T.V. WATCHDOG
TERRY RAKOLTA)

LYNCHBURG, VA.
(HOME OF JERRY FALWELL)

DISNEYWORLD

TUPELO, MISS.
(HOME OF THE AMERICAN
FAMILY ASSOCIATION)

DUBUQUE, IOWA
(THE LITTLE OLD
LADY FOR
WHOM THE
NEW YORKER
IS NOT INTENDED
HAILS FROM
HERE.)

KILGORE, TX
(HOME OF THE
EMINENTLY WHOLESOME
RANGERETTES)

SALT LAKE
CITY, UTAH

GARDEN GROVE, CA.
(HOME OF ROBERT
SCHULER'S CRYSTAL CATHEDRAL)

had not yet become pimples on the landscape. And everywhere, even in cities, the air was fresh and unsullied.

Nowadays, however, it's not that simple. Corporate prigs must reside where their employer stations them. Professional prigs must reside within commuting distance of their offices. Consequently, there are prigs who live in such unlikely places as Marin County, California, and in the heart of darkness on Manhattan's Lower East Side. There are prigs who live within spitting distance of the decadent Kennedy family in Massachusetts, and on New Orleans' St. Charles Avenue—less than a three-second drive from the sinful, salacious French quarter. There are prigs who live on farms, in skyscrapers, and in solar-powered Vermont chalets.

The recent boom in mail-order shopping has liberated prigs to live wherever they must. From their Williams-Sonoma catalogs, they can have such essentials as extra-virgin olive oil and surgical steel cookware delivered anywhere: from downtown Dallas to the Alaskan tundra. From their L. L. Bean and J. Crew catalogs, they can obtain sensible, well-constructed, blessedly fashion-free clothes. And thanks to Hammacher Schlemmer, any cutting-edge gadget obtainable in big-city stores is just as available in northern Nova Scotia.

Prigs who reside in gentrified urban neighborhoods may feel obliged to patronize their local health food emporium or organic grocer, but even they often shop by mail. It's so much more pleasant than visiting stores: cleaner, quieter, more efficient, and more discreet. In time, I predict, it will supplant the vulgarity of the marketplace. Ultimately, prigdom isn't a geopolitical state; it's a state of mind.

Ralph Nader

Hard to believe, but this dinosaur consumer activist and author of *Unsafe at Any Speed* is still living on what amounts to a graduate student's wages while tilting against the windmills of corporate injustice. Ironically, however, his recent campaign to prevent a pay raise for Congress placed him squarely on the side of big business—ensuring that lawmakers, unable to make ends meet, could continue to be bought cheaply by special interests.

How to Drive Like a Prig

No matter where they live or how they shop, prigs must venture out into the world sometime. And when they do, they go like everyone else—in the family car.

Prig drivers prefer to sit in the seat next to the one behind the steering wheel. In this position, it's nearly impossible to make a mistake. On those occasions, however, when they must travel alone, you'll find them swathed in seat belts behind the wheel of last year's *Consumer Reports'* crash tests winner.

Prigs fasten the seat belts in the back of taxis. They would never dream of riding in a convertible. They're even lobbying to have them banned again. And not even policemen, they believe, should ride motorcycles: the practice sets a bad example for children.

Prigs are opposed to the 55 mph speed limit; they'd prefer to see it lowered to 35 mph or even 25 mph. Despite their aversion to traveling at even a moderate clip, however, they usually position themselves in the middle or far left lanes. This is to prevent others from traveling at even a moderate clip.

These seven questions should help you gauge your potential as a road prig:

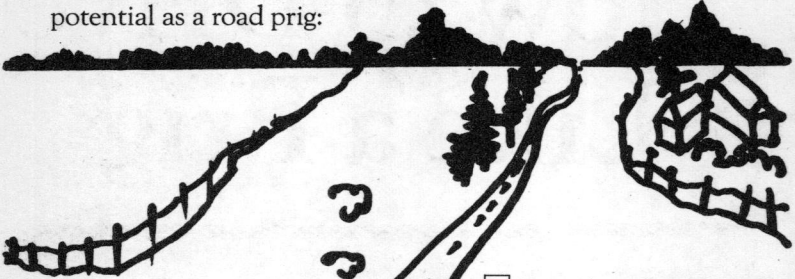

1 Say you find yourself driving 10 mph below the speed limit in the fast lane of a major expressway. Do you...

a) increase your pace to keep up with the flow of traffic?

b) slow down — and tap your brake pedal to torment the Porsche in back of you?

c) dial the police on your cellular phone to give them the license number of the Chevy that roared past you on the right?

2 Complete this sentence. *When I'm in a school zone I...*
a. slow to 25 mph.
b. slow to 15 mph.
c. pull over and park until sunset when the kids have gone home and it's safe to drive.

3 The penalty for driving while intoxicated should be....   a. suspension of license.
b. revocation of license.
c. death.

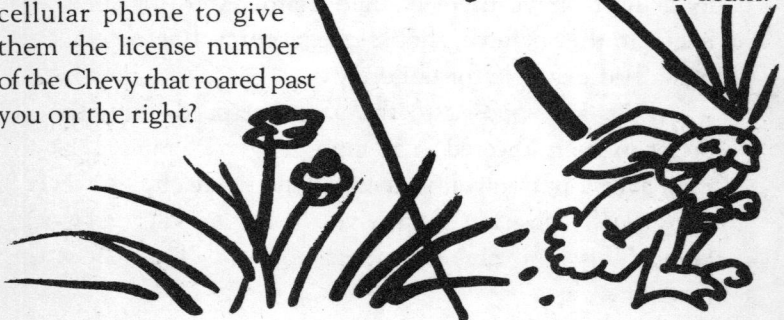

4 I believe child seats should be mandatory...
a. in cars.
b. on planes.
c. in rocking chairs.

5 If you find yourself riding with a driver who speeds, do you...
a. say nothing?
b. say the rosary?
c. discuss how your cousin Cheryl became a quadriplegic after sustaining a cervical fracture in a minor fender bender?

6 If you are riding with a driver who runs a red light, do you...
a. suggest he receive treatment for color-blindness?
b. suggest he is a danger to himself and others?
c. suggest he pull to the side of the road so you can get out and walk?

7 And finally, my idea of a hot car is...
a. my neighbor's Miata.
b. my father's Oldsmobile.
c. any car that previously belonged to my father.

If you answered "a" to any of these questions, you're in big trouble. Such answers indicate a wild, reckless streak that will have to be tamed. You might want to trade in your Corvette for a Ford Escort or have your engine adapted so that it can't run faster than 75 mph. And if that doesn't work, use public transportation.

Accessories
and Gifts

Although a baby is a prig couple's ultimate accessory, many married prigs must wait a few years before successfully producing one. Some couples in that predicament—to say nothing of their single counterparts—choose to fill their lives with dogs, cats, Cuisinarts, CD players, and other diversions. Many prig parents also enjoy animals: they're much more appreciative and adoring than selfish, willful children.

Prigs do not own exotic, marginal pets—cobras, monkeys, geckos, kangaroo rats, or South American parrots. Nor do they own decadent, long-haired cats. Some prigs, usually elderly spinsters or book editors, develop attachments to short-haired felines, but an allergy to cats occurs more frequently in prigs than in the general population.

By and large, prigs prefer dogs. Dogs share with their owners a similar temperament: a lack of independence and a willingness to accept orders. They are steadfast, loyal, and contemptuous of spicy food. Not only are they xenophobic, but they can be trained to attack strangers who threaten either their owners or their owners' possessions. If they could only be taught to clean up the messes they leave on the street, they would be perfect.

Perhaps you're wondering: What kind of dogs are a prig's best friend?

a. drug-sniffing German shepherds?

b. Shih Tzus, Yorkshire terriers, any dog with a tight topknot?

c. Dogs that button all the buttons on their sweaters?

d. All of the above?

The correct answer, as you have no doubt guessed, is "d."

When a prig's birthday or special occasion arises, accessories make excellent gifts. Filofaxes or engraved fountain pens (never ballpoint or felt-tip) are sure to delight the prigs in your life. Prigs themselves frequently give one another those dried fruit samplers that are delivered once a month for a year to remind the recipient of the giver's generosity. Other favorites include surgical steel toenail parers; non–gender-specific, bulky-knit sweaters made from the wool of animals who live above the timberline; high-speed ergonomic hand calculators; ultraviolet toothbrush sanitizers; home water distillers; and—the ultimate prig product—unscented cologne.

If you have ambivalent (or even hostile) feelings about the prig for whom you must select a gift, consider bringing him or her a cuddly, long-haired kitten. Or lavish any of these presents upon his or her children: a box of Godiva chocolates, a sexually explicit Judy Blume novel, a Ronald McDonald gift certificate, or the complete *Rambo* video library.

Phyllis Schlafly

For more than twenty years, this Harvard-educated housewife, mother, and ERA opponent from Alton, Illinois, has fought to keep women barefoot and pregnant. And despite her own expensively shod feet and well-planned family, she has more or less succeeded.

Jiang Qing

Jiang Qing began her career as the youthful model-actress wife of an older political figure, Chinese Communist Party leader Mao Tse-tung. She shaped taste and style in the People's Republic by initiating the "Cultural Revolution"—a ruthless purge of any and all people tainted by Western capitalism. After Mao's death, however, the murderous aspects of her ideological fastidiousness lost popular support, and she was executed for treason along with the other members of the notorious "Gang of Four."

"Dear Miss Priss"

Sometimes unforeseen pitfalls cause even the staunchest of prigs to trip up. When this happens, it's time to consult Miss Priss. You may not like her advice, but she's almost never wrong.

Dear Miss Priss:

I'm being persecuted because I'm beautiful, I like nice things, and I have a devoted husband. So what if I demand a great deal of my staff! What's more, some of those little people resent me just because I have money—though, God knows, I worked for every cent of it. What price high standards?

Leona Helmsley, Queen
New York City

Your Majesty: About $70 million, according to the IRS. Miss Priss has every confidence that you labored long and hard for your money— she's still rather in doubt, however, about what exactly it was that you did. She is certain, however, that three years behind bars will only enhance your gracious, generous, fastidious nature—and hopes you will make every effort to maintain the same high standards in your correctional facility that you do in your hotels.

Dear Miss Priss:

I am a shy woman and I cannot discuss this problem with any of the other ladies in our local Republican Flower Arranging and Village Improvement Club.

I tremble to realize that no other married woman has probably ever suffered from my dilemma, but my husband—a hardworking, God-fearing provider—cannot postpone his pleasure. Our conjugal relations take less time than is required to boil an egg. And they are very untidy to boot.

I turn to you, Miss Priss, a stranger, for help.

Name Withheld in
Prairie City, Minnesota

Dear Name Withheld: Having no personal experience with your predicament, let me refer you to a remark sometimes attributed the ever-eloquent Noël Coward: "Lash it to a toothbrush."

Dear Miss Priss:

Recently, vile out driving, I vas harassed by a police officer and accused of striking him. I vas subjected to a humiliating trial—and ze prying lenses of a thousand TV cameras. Now ze public accuses me of exploiting ze incident to promote my career. What can I do to stop zis slander?

> Zsa Zsa Gabor, actress
> Beverly Hills

Dear Miss Gabor: Eastern Europe has become quite fashionable this year. Have you considered re-immigrating?

Dear Miss Priss:

I am married to a cleaning fanatic. No sooner do we begin to make love than she yanks the sheets off of the bed and tosses them into the Maytag.

Her behavior is so bizarre that I've had no recourse but to withdraw into the the tawdry embraces of my secretary—a state of affairs of which, as Moose Club president and occasional alderman, I am not proud.

I'm also worried about my health: my secretary has recently developed an unseemly rash whose outline has begun to assume for me the shape of a scarlet A. How can I extricate myself from this sticky situation?

Guilty in
Prairie City, Minnesota

Dear Guilty: As quickly as possible. And you should be worried about your health—your mental health. I urge you to get professional help: most well-adjusted men prefer a clean bed to a bed of filth.

Dear Miss Priss:

After my wife and I began divorce proceedings, I discovered that I was irresistible to women. It is really all I can do each day to beat the hordes of them from my doorstep.

What's more, I'm certain that the vast majority are AIDS-ridden and herpetic—planted by my enemies to infect my perfect body with diseases.

There is, however, one clean and innocent young model/actress who has touched my heart. Before I allow her to touch the rest of me, how can I make sure she is as clean and innocent as she appears?

Donald Trump, rich person
New York City

Dear Mr. Trump: Insist on a thorough examination by your personal physician. And if you are considering concubinage on a grander scale, it might be cost-efficient to set up an HMO or similar group plan for your model/actresses.

Dear Miss Priss:

Perhaps this may shock you, but my lover is a married man, and though I blush at the cliché, he is also my boss.

This is not, however, my problem. My problem is I am allergic to him or to his laundry soap. It began with a few sniffles and sneezes that responded to antihistamines, but last week I broke out in a rash.

He has threatened to go back to his wife if it doesn't clear up. Frankly, Miss Priss, I don't see his problem. I'm willing to live with a hideous disfigurement for him. But alas, he is so fastidious that he must readjust his boutonniere after each tryst under his mahogany desk.

Should I consult a dermatologist in another city? Or stand firm in my conviction that a woman has a right to do what she wants with her own body?

Blotchy in
Prairie City, Minnesota

Dear Blotchy: Ever hear the expression "Form follows function"? If you look disgusting, perhaps it is a reflection of your behavior. Wash that man right out of your hair and your skin will follow suit.

Dear Miss Priss:

    Recently I fell—and fell hard—for Mr. Wrong. My life has been a shambles ever since—trials, more lawyers than I can count, and everywhere I turn, photographers. Miss Priss, I've become an object of ridicule. What can I do to regain my dignity?

Bess Myerson, former Miss America
New York City

Dear Miss America: Implore God for strength. Vanessa Williams triumphed over a similar lapse in judgment and so will you.

Dear Miss Priss:

I am worried about a friend in my garden club. Her usually elegant flower arrangements have deteriorated into—how shall I say this?—pornographic sprays of enormous proportions.

She has also withdrawn from her friends. We know that her husband has succumbed to the slovenly, unkempt advances of one of his employees. Should we tell her? Would it help raise the standards of her floral arrangements once more?

> Worried in
> Prairie City, Minnesota

Dear Worried: As Miss Priss understands it, standards are not the thing your friend has to fret about raising. Concern yourselves with the stamens and pistils in your own gardens.

Dear Miss Priss:

About ten years ago, I accidentally shot and killed my beloved while attempting to commit suicide. He was an excellent doctor and a wonderful man. Since that dark day, I've stood trial, served most of my sentence, written two books, and worked to extend the rights of convicts who are mothers. I've also suffered extreme remorse. I feel I deserve to be pardoned. How can I convince Governor Mario Cuomo that I'm no longer a threat to society?

> Jean Harris
> Bedford Hills, New York

Dear Mrs. Harris: Threat to society? Miss Priss thinks you're a jewel. After reading the details of your trial, she believes Dr. Herman Tarnower was a promiscuous skunk who richly deserved what he got. Miss Priss will personally lobby the governor for your pardon. And consider yourself on the short list for her annual Good Riddance to Bad Rubbish Neighborhood Clean-up Award.

The Ayatollah Khomeini

In the revolution of 1979, this celebrated hostage-taker and religious fanatic restored the fear of God and propriety in ladies' dress to Iran, a country that had fallen into decadence under the rule of the satanic, U.S.-supported shah. In later years, he attempted a second career as a literary critic, but his opinions were not universally well-received.

Jerry Falwell

Founder and head of the now-defunct Moral Majority, the Reverend Falwell was among the first televangelists to broadcast the gospel according to Ronald Reagan. By keeping his fly shut and his mind closed, Falwell rose above the Elmer Gantry-esque scandals of the late 80s—effectively disassociating himself from theme-park Christians Jimmy and Tammy Bakker and Jimmy "Look But Don't Touch" Swaggart.

The Prig Way of Death

Considering their obsession with cleanliness, it's not surprising that neo-prigs strive to sanitize death. Death mocks their way of life. More potent than oat bran, swifter than a state-of-the-art running shoe, death catches up with their bodies and reduces them to dust.

Neo-prigs struggle to ignore this fact. When one of their number departs, they promptly whisk his or her body off to the crematorium. Later, when the ashes have been scattered and there is no physical reminder of the body, they may eulogize their loved one. But such eulogizing will occur in a memorial service that, even if conducted in a religious setting, is so sterile as to be secular.

Neo-prigs do not wail, gnash their teeth, throw themselves onto open caskets, or even acknowledge what has taken place. They deny, rather than grieve. They jog, rather than weep.

Ironically, traditional prigs have a much healthier attitude toward death. They understand its importance and cope with it through ritual. They sit *shiva*, mourn, and break their vows of temperance at wakes. They *grieve*.

For, to traditional prigs, death is the goal of life, not something to be avoided. Death is the ultimate reward: the reason they avoid "sin" in life. Whereas, for neo-prigs, death is the ultimate punishment: they avoid "sin" to avoid death.

I can't in good conscience counsel you to emulate the neo-prigs at funerals. It's too unhealthy—not to mention inhuman and life-denying. On the bright side, however, this denial of death may become their undoing.

To acknowledge birth and death is to recognize that life advances in cycles: beings come into the world, live their lives, and depart. Likewise, in the opinion of some historians, social movements come into the world, take hold, and pass away.

Traditional prigs will probably always be with us. But the neo-prig fad, I suspect, is destined to wane. When this happens, I look forward to one h-ll of a party.

Andy Warhol

Warhol himself may have indulged in a decadent life-style financed by depraved rich people, but in *The Warhol Diaries*—published posthumously—the artist indicted all of them: Margaret Trudeau, Liza Minnelli, and Bianca Jagger are portrayed as drug-hungry has-beens; Studio 54 as the black hole of cocaine; and the writers and actors of his acquaintance as promiscuous, no-talent clothes racks. Long after his pictures have faded and his films have crumbled into dust, his diary will endure—the white-powder generation's Pepys.

M. G. (nee Mary Grace) Lord spent her childhood amid the fleshpots of Southern California and currently resides in Greenwich Village, another cesspool of moral turpitude, where she is a syndicated columnist and political cartoonist based at *New York Newsday*. Her vices include raising cats, drinking coffee, and collecting Evelyn Waugh first editions, an activity in which she is aided and abetted by her husband, a rare book and manuscript dealer.